The Railway Rabbits

Barley and the Duck Race

The Railway Rabbits

Barley and the Duck Race

Georgie Adams

Illustrated by Anna Currey

Orion
Children's Books

First published in Great Britain in 2012
by Orion Children's Books
This edition published in 2014
by Orion Children's Books
a division of the Orion Publishing Group Ltd
Orion House, 5 Upper St Martin's Lane
London WC2H 9EA
An Hachette UK company

1 3 5 7 9 10 8 6 4 2

A catalogue record for this book is available from the British Library.

ISBN 978 1 4440 1222 4

Printed in Great Britain by Clays Ltd, St Ives plc

www.orionbooks.co.uk
www.georgieadams.com

For Laura, Imogen and Neil
– with love G.A

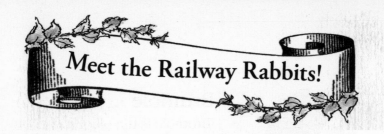

Meet the Railway Rabbits!

Wisher Longears

The smallest of the
Longears children,
Wisher has silvery-white
fur and pink ears.
She wears a kerchief
around her neck.

Personality: Quiet and thoughtful, but
with an adventurous side. When something
unusual is about to happen, her ears tingle!

Likes: Exploring, mysteries, her best friend,
Parsley Mole.

Dislikes: People-folk, being the centre of
attention because of her special powers.

Favourite saying: "My ears are tingling!"

Bramble Longears

Bramble is the biggest and bossiest of the rabbits. He has a shiny, jet-black coat, and wears a stripy scarf.

Personality: A fearless and adventurous rabbit, Bramble loves to be the leader and is very competitive.

Likes: Winning races, playing with his friends Tansy and Teasel.

Dislikes: Losing to his brother Bracken, not being the leader.

Favourite saying: "Wriggly worms!"

Bracken Longears

Bracken has pale, gingery-brown fur and ears with black tips. He wears a spotty kerchief around his neck.

Personality: Like Bramble, he loves adventure, but isn't quite as brave as his brother. He's the fastest, though, and always wins races!

Likes: Running fast, working out problems without Bramble's help, his friend Nigel.

Dislikes: Not being in charge.

Favourite saying: "Slugs and snails!"

Berry Longears

Berry has a reddish-brown coat with white tail, tummy and paws. He wears a jacket.

Personality: Berry can always be relied on to cheer everyone up with a joke. He is always falling over and getting himself into trouble.

Likes: Corncobs, jokes and Fern, his favourite sister.

Dislikes: Monsters, especially the beasts that hide in the maze at Fairweather's Farm Park.

Favourite saying: "Creeping caterpillars!"

Fern Longears

Fern has a soft grey coat with fern-like black markings between her ears, a white tummy and two front paws. She wears a daisy chain around her neck.

Personality: Fern is a worrier and often assumes the worst will happen, but she is also inquisitive, creative and good at finding things.

Likes: Stories, singing, hunting for pretty shiny objects.

Dislikes: Owls, rats and any kind of danger to herself and her brothers and sisters.

Favourite saying: "Bugs and beetles!"

Mellow Longears

Mellow has grey-brown
fur, a white nose and
big, soft eyes. She wears
a straw hat decorated
with flowers.

Personality: Sensible and well-organised.
She loves all her children, but pays special
attention to Wisher, who needs extra
protection because of her gift.

Likes: Flowers, chatting to her friends
Daisy Duck and Sylvia Squirrel.

Dislikes: Silliness, untidiness and the Red
Dragon.

Favourite saying: "Silly rabbits have
careless habits."

Barley Longears

Barley has black and white fur, and unusually long ears. He wears a waistcoat with barley straws in his pocket.

Personality: A real worrier! Barley cares about his family, and spends most of his time keeping a sharp watch for trouble.

Likes: His favourite look-out tree stump, his best friend Blinker Badger.

Dislikes: Burdock the Buzzard.

Favourite saying: "Oh, buttercups!"

THE LONGEARS / SILVERCOAT FAMILIES

BARLEYCORN LONGEARS
OF DEEP BURROW
GREAT ~ GREAT ~ ELDER PARR

MEADOW SILVERCOAT
OF CASTLE HILL
AND GREAT ~ GREAT ~ ELDER MARR

|

BUTTERWORT LONGEARS
& POPPY
GREAT ~ ELDER PARR
& GREAT ~ ELDER MARR
LONGEARS

WOODRUFF SILVERCOAT
& MALLOW
GREAT ~ ELDER PARR
& GREAT ~ ELDER MARR
SILVERCOAT

|

BLACKBERRY LONGEARS
& PRIMROSE
ELDER PARR & ELDER MARR
LONGEARS

EYEBRIGHT SILVERCOAT
& WILLOW
ELDER PARR & ELDER MARR
SILVERCOAT

BARLEY LONGEARS AND MELLOW SILVERCOAT
PARR AND MARR

|

BRAMBLE   BRACKEN   BERRY   FERN   WISHER
BUCK   BUCK   BUCK   DOE   DOE

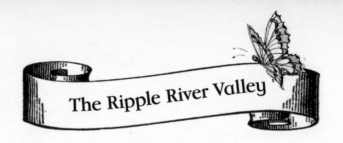

The Ripple River Valley

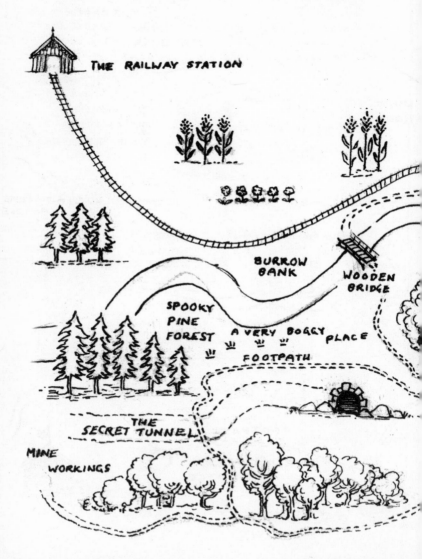

THE RAILWAY STATION

BURROW BANK

WOODEN BRIDGE

SPOOKY PINE FOREST

A VERY BOGGY PLACE

FOOTPATH

THE SECRET TUNNEL

MINE WORKINGS

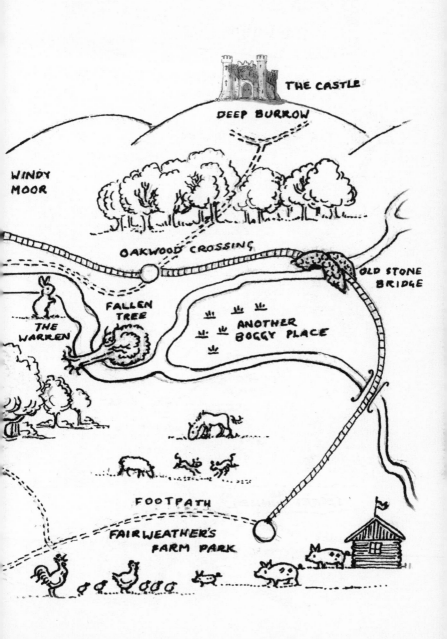

A Dash and a Splash

1

One warm spring day, Barley Longears poked his head out of the burrow and took a deep breath. His nose twitched with excitement at the scents around him.

"Ah!" said Barley. "The grass smells sweet. The air smells good. Everything smells wonderful this morning!" He called down the tunnel to his family. "Come on. It's great to be up-burrow!"

Mellow and the five young Longears rabbits hurried along a narrow passageway, then up a slope and out into the sunshine. Mellow stretched her legs and felt the sun warm on her back. The three bucks were close behind – glossy black Bramble, gingery Bracken, and Berry with his reddish-brown fur. Berry looked to see where the does had got to.

"Come on, you two. You're as slow as snails!"

"Coming!" said Fern, running from the tunnel after him. She had a soft, grey coat with black wisps of hair between her ears.

Last came Wisher, the smallest of them all. She hopped from the burrow entrance and shook her silvery-white fur. Everyone busied themselves finding plants and seeds to eat nearby.

"Mmm!" said Mellow, nibbling a juicy dandelion. "I think spring is my favourite time of year."

"I agree," said Barley, munching a mouthful of leaves.

He waggled his unusually long ears. "Listen! The birds are singing at the tops of their voices."

"I expect they're building new nests," said Mellow.

After a while, Berry got bored. He sat up and pulled a funny face, which made Bramble, Bracken, Fern and Wisher laugh. When he was sure he'd got their attention, he said, "Watch this." He took three long leaps, bounced once, then flipped a backwards somersault.

Unfortunately, Berry lost his balance and landed on his nose with a *bump!* "Ouch!" he said. "That hurt."

"Oh dear," said Mellow. "Trust you to do something silly!"

She gave him a hug and rubbed his sore nose.

Berry soon felt better and gave everyone a cheeky grin.

"What shall we do now?" said Bramble.

"Race you to the wooden bridge," said Bracken.

"You'll win," said Wisher.

"You always do," said Fern. "You're the fastest."

"Hm?" said Bramble. "We'll see about that." He didn't want Bracken to win again. He liked to be best at everything. "This time, I'll be first! One, two, three – GO."

"Hey!" said Bracken. "I wasn't ready."

"It's not fair," said Fern.

"Come back," said Berry.

"Wait for me," said Wisher.

"Stay where we can see you,"
said Mellow.

"Don't get up to mischief!" said Barley.

"Yes, Marr! Yes, Parr!" the four young
rabbits cried.

Barley and Mellow watched
them chase after Bramble. Then Mellow
sat down to groom her grey-brown fur.

"I'll keep a look-out for trouble," said Barley, and he went away to his favourite tree stump. It was a good place to watch for dangerous animals like foxes and stoats, and Barley's number one enemy – Burdock the buzzard!

When he got to the stump, Barley checked the telegraph pole. He knew it was where Burdock often sat, waiting to catch a rabbit. But, to Barley's relief, the bird was nowhere to be seen.

"Thank goodness!" he said. "Burdock must be hunting somewhere else today."

The sun rose in the sky. Barley heard a bee buzzing in a clump of clover. The *buzz-buzz-buzz* of the bee made him feel sleepy. He was just dozing off when two large birds flew down. They had blue-black feathers and sharp, shiny beaks. Barley thought they looked fierce. He watched them gathering some twigs, until they saw him and hopped over. Oh, buttercups! thought Barley.

The birds cocked their heads and looked at Barley with their beady eyes.

"Hello," said one. "I'm Clary Crow."

"I'm Craggs Crow," said the other.

The birds seemed friendly so Barley introduced himself.

"Barley Longears," he said. "Do you live around here?"

"Yes," said Clary. "We've made a nest in the big oak."

"We used to live in the wood near Fairweather's," said Craggs. "But our old home was destroyed by a fire."

"Ah," said Barley. "I remember that day. A dreadful business! There was smoke everywhere. You must have been very frightened. Welcome to this part of the valley. By the way, my burrow is over there . . ."

"Longears!" said Clary suddenly. "We met a small white rabbit on the day of the fire, didn't we, Craggs? I think she said her name was Longears . . ."

"Wisher Longears!" said Craggs. "A funny little thing. She said her ears were trying to tell her something."

"Wisher is my youngest doe," said Barley proudly. "Her ears tingle and she hears voices. Wisher knows things before they happen."

"Caw!" said Clary. "How clever! I wonder if Wisher knows about the strange bird we saw this morning?"

"What bird?" said Barley. "Where?"

"It was standing in the river on long, thin legs," said Craggs.

Barley would have liked to know more but, suddenly, he heard *thump, thump, thump!* It was the sound of a rabbit's foot thumping the ground, the warning signal he knew so well. Barley looked around nervously.

At first he couldn't see anything. Then he saw Mellow pointing to the sky and heard her calling: "Bramble, Bracken, Berry, Fern, Wisher. Burdock! Watch out!"

To Barley's horror, he saw the buzzard hovering high above the wooden bridge where his young rabbits were playing.

"My children are in danger!" said
Barley. "I must protect them. Goodbye!"

"Brave rabbit," said Craggs. "Maybe
we'll have children too, one day?"

"Maybe," said Clary. "Come on. Let's
finish building our new nest."

Bramble, Bracken, Berry, Fern and
Wisher were playing hide-and-seek.
When it was Wisher's turn to seek the
others went to hide, leaving Wisher alone
by the wooden bridge.

Bramble hid behind a tree.

Bracken hid under a hedge.

Berry and Fern were hiding by a holly bush, until Berry trod on a prickly leaf.

"Ow, ow, ow!" he said, hopping around on one foot.

Fern giggled.

"Ssh!" she said. "Wisher will know where we are."

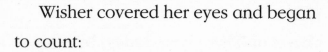

Wisher covered her eyes and began
to count:

"One, two, three . . ."

She stopped. Her ears were tingling
– a sure sign that something was about
to happen. She wanted to peep between
her paws, but she thought that wouldn't
be fair. If Bramble, Bracken, Berry and
Fern saw, they would think she was

cheating! Wisher carried on
counting:

"Five, six, seven . . ."
Her ears tingled
again and she could
hear a voice inside
her head. Only she
couldn't make out
the words.

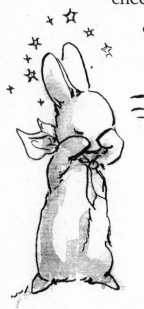

I wonder what it's trying to say? thought
Wisher. Then she finished counting:

"Eight, nine . . . TEN! Coming!"

Wisher felt the ground vibrate. It
was a rabbit's foot urgently pounding
a warning.

Thump, thump, thump!

She heard Marr shout, and saw
her pointing to the sky. Wisher looked
up. A split-second later, Burdock was
speeding towards her. Wisher froze. She
didn't know what to do! Then she heard
Bramble cry:

"Wisher! Watch out!"

At the same time, she caught a glimpse of something moving fast. A blur of black and white fur dashing towards the bridge. It was Parr! Next thing she knew, Parr was flinging himself between her and the buzzard. Burdock flew up with a startled screech.

It was Berry and Fern who saw Barley fall headfirst into the river.

"Parr couldn't stop," said Berry.

"He was going too fast," said Fern.

"Parr saved me from Burdock!" said Wisher, trembling with shock. "I knew my ears were trying to tell me something!"

But when they looked for Barley, he was nowhere to be seen.

SPLASH! Down, down, down. Barley sank to the bottom of the river like a stone. The water was icy cold and bubbled around his ears. He felt slimy mud ooze between his paws.

"Ugh!" cried Barley, and got a mouthful of muddy water. He began to panic. I can't breathe. I need air! He paddled with his paws, trying to reach the surface. But his fur was wet and it was weighing him down. I'm going to drown! thought Barley.

Then he touched something and Barley grabbed it. It was too dark to see what it was, but it felt like a thin stick. And there was another! Two sticks, standing side by side in the mud. Just what I need, thought Barley, and he began to climb them.

Barley couldn't remember what came next, because everything happened so quickly. To his surprise, the sticks shot up through the water and into the air!

Barley held on for his life, wondering what was going on. It was then he discovered his mistake. He was clinging to the legs of an enormous bird.

"Help! Help!" cried Barley.
"Put me down!"

All
Aboard!
2

That same morning the cats, Florence and Skittles, were sitting on the platform of the Ripple Valley Steam Railway Station. The big red engine SPITFIRE Number 47512 was hissing and puffing, ready to be off. It was attached to three carriages, and these were nearly full.

"Lots of passengers today," said Florence. "More than usual."

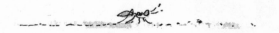

"Yes," said Skittles. "And there's something else. Most of them have pets. So far I've counted eight dogs, six rabbits, two guinea pigs and . . ."

"Mice!" said Florence with a wicked glint in her eye. She had spotted a little boy carrying three white mice in a cage. "I wonder what's going on?"

"Well," said Skittles, "there's only one way to find out. Let's jump aboard and see. The children look very excited. We can listen to what they say."

Florence looked worried.

"What if the train goes while we're on it?" she said.

"We'll have a train ride, that's what!" said Skittles brightly. "I did it once before, remember?"

"Yes," said Florence. "I thought I'd never see you again!"

"Trust me," said Skittles. "Train rides are fun. And I know the Timetable like the back of my paws. The train goes down the line to Fairweather's Farm Park, then back again. It runs twice before lunchtime. The same again before tea. We'll be home before anyone notices we're missing."

Florence admired the way Skittles
knew everything there was to know
about the railway. She loved him and
thought he was very clever.

"All right," she said. "I'll come."

"It will be an adventure," said Skittles.

The cats walked down the platform
and stopped at the third carriage.

"Purrfect!" said Skittles. "This one has open sides, and benches for the passengers to sit on. We can hide under a seat."

No one took any notice of the two cats – one black, one tabby – until a dog called Toby spotted them. Toby had ridden on the train before and knew Florence and Skittles lived at the Station. He barked a friendly greeting.

"Woof! Woof!"

"Sshh!" said Florence. "We're not supposed to be here."

Toby looked puzzled.

"I thought you were going to the Pet Show at the Farm Park?" he said.

"Er, not exactly," said Florence.

"What's a Pet Show?" said Skittles.

"Ha! Don't you know?" said Toby. "People-folk go to Pet Shows to show off their pets. They hope to win prizes. All of my friends are going. I'm entered for the Tail-Wagging competition. My mistress says she's sure I'll win First Prize. I never stop wagging my tail!"

"What are prizes?" said Florence.

"Are they good to eat?" said Skittles.

Toby was about to explain when George, the station master, walked by.

"All aboard!" cried George.

He waved his flag and blew
his whistle.

"We're off!" said Skittles.

"Uh-oh," said Florence. She wasn't
sure this was such a good idea after all.
But before she could change her mind,
the train began to move. Then it went
rattling down the line, gathering speed.

Clickerty-clack. Clickerty-click!

"Ooo!" said Florence. "We're going very fast. The trees and hedges are whizzing by."

"Hold on tight!" said Skittles.

Suddenly, SPITFIRE let out a piercing shriek.

Whooo-Wheeep!

Then they went into a tunnel.

"Oh!" cried Florence. "What's happening?"

Just as suddenly, they rushed from the tunnel and out into bright sunshine again.

"That was SO scary!" said Florence.

"I was a bit frightened too," said Toby.

"It was only a tunnel," said Skittles. "Don't worry. There isn't another. We'll soon be arriving at Fairweather's."

Skittles was settling down to enjoy the rest of the journey when something caught his eye. It was the most extraordinary sight! Some children had spotted it too and were pointing to the sky.

"Look, Florence," said Skittles. "A flying rabbit!"

"You see some funny things from a train," said Florence.

Barley
Goes
Flying
3

Hazel Heron took off in fright. She had been standing in the River Ripple for some time, patiently waiting for a fish. She had been about to catch one when a rabbit dived into the water. Then, to her great surprise, it grabbed her legs! Hazel couldn't believe what was happening. She'd never known anything like it.

"Oh, my beak and feathers!" she cried.

Hazel flapped her large, grey wings. She tried to take off, but the rabbit held on. He was very heavy! Hazel beat her wings harder.

Flap, flap, flap!

Then, after a lot of effort, she flew out of the water. *Flap, flap, flap!* Up in the air, but still the rabbit clung tight. What can I do? thought Hazel. This rabbit won't let go!

Barley was so scared he thought his tail
would drop off. They flew over hedges.
Over tree-tops! Barley closed his eyes.
When he opened them again, the
ground looked a long way away. The
wind whistled past his ears. He felt sick.
He didn't know how much longer he
could hold on. If I fall, he
thought, I'll die!

Just when
Barley thought
things couldn't
get any worse,
they did. The
bird flew higher!

"Stop!" cried Barley. "Please, stop. Put
me DOWN!"

He tried to shout, but he couldn't.
Barley's words were no more than a
whisper. His paws ached and he could
hardly feel them. When he began to slip,
Barley gripped the bird's legs tighter. I
must hold on, he thought. I can't let go . . .

Hazel Heron saw a puff of smoke and
heard a whistle.

Whooo-Wheeep!

The Red Dragon! Hazel was getting
tired. The rabbit was weighing her down.

I must find somewhere safe to land,
she thought, away from the Red Dragon's
tracks. But I can't fly much further.

Oh, what can I do? I've tried to get rid of this rabbit, but he won't let go!

Suddenly, Hazel spotted the Farm Park. She knew it well.

"I'll make for the duck pond," she said. "With any luck, I can drop this rabbit in there!"

Hazel swooped low. Barley's stomach churned.

"HELP! HELP!" he cried.

This time Hazel heard him. She was amazed.

"First you attack me," she said. "Now you want my help!"

But Hazel was flying too fast to change course. A moment later – SPLASH! She landed right in the middle of the duck pond.

"Glug-glug-glug!" spluttered Barley, underwater for the second time that day.

"Quack, quack, quack!" went Daisy Duck, who happened to be swimming there. She was very surprised to see Barley Longears so far from home.

The pond wasn't very deep and Barley crawled up the muddy bank.

"This is the worst day of my life!" he said.

"Barley!" said Daisy. "What are you doing with Hazel Heron?"

"That rabbit tried to catch me," said Hazel crossly. "He wouldn't let go."

"What?" said Daisy. "Are you sure, Hazel? Barley is a good friend of mine. There must be some mistake."

"Yes," said Barley, wringing water from his ears. "Please, let me explain. I was trying to protect Wisher from Burdock the buzzard. I was running and fell in the river . . ."

"Oh," said Hazel. "I see."

"What a story!" said Daisy. "And Wisher? Did you save her, Barley?"

"I don't know," said Barley. "I think she got away. Oh, I hope she's all right. I must get back."

Hazel felt sorry for Barley. She could see now it had all been a big misunderstanding. Water dripped from his coat, and there was a puddle at his feet. He looked very miserable.

"Shall I take you home?" she said. "I think I could manage to fly, though you are quite heavy."

"Oh, er, no thanks," said Barley quickly. "It's very kind of you, Hazel. But I prefer to keep my paws firmly on the ground!"

"Well, goodbye," said Hazel. "Now, I must catch some fish. I'm hungry after all that flying! Maybe we'll meet again soon."

"Maybe," said Barley. "Goodbye!"

Barley and Daisy watched Hazel fly to the river. Then a shrill whistle caught their attention.

Whooo-Wheeep!

"The Red Dragon!" said Barley.

They looked towards the tracks, which ran close to the Farm Park. Sure enough, the monster was puffing along, belching clouds of smoke. A few minutes later, they saw it slow down, then stop at Fairweather's Halt.

"The Dragon has brought lots of people-folk," said Barley. "They're brave to ride on his back."

"It's a special day at Fairweather's," said Daisy. "Everyone's come for the Pet Show. There's a Duck Race too."

"A Duck Race?" said Barley. "What's that about?"

"I have no idea," said Daisy. "But I've seen some very strange ducks around this morning. Yellow ones. Quite a few! They're not very friendly. I spoke to one, but he didn't say a word!"

Barley was keeping one eye on the people-folk. A small crowd had gathered on the grass with their pets. He saw:

A boy with white mice,

a little girl carrying a rabbit with droopy, black ears,

two cats by themselves,

and some dogs.

"Oh, buttercups!' said Barley. "Dogs! I've had enough trouble for one day. Which is the quickest way home, Daisy?"

"Along the riverbank," said Daisy. "I'll come with you. I'm not staying here with those strange-looking ducks!"

Quack, quack, quack!

Prizes
at the
Pet Show
4

Barley and Daisy made their way to the
riverbank. Suddenly, they heard a dog
barking:

Woof! Woof! Woof!

Barley froze. He was afraid of dogs almost as much as he was afraid of Burdock the buzzard. A long-haired dog bounded towards them, yelping excitedly. Then Barley panicked. He ran.

"Stop! Stop!" quacked Daisy to the dog. Daisy knew Sasha. She was the young sheepdog who lived at Fairweather's Farm Park. "That's Barley . . ."

But Sasha was much too excited to listen to a duck. She raced after Barley, nose down, sniffing. This is fun! she thought.

Barley darted this way and that, looking for somewhere to hide – a bush, a hole, anywhere!

The dog was close on his tail. He could hear it panting. Barley's heart thumped. He stopped to catch his breath. Then he heard someone shout:

"Come here!"

Before Barley knew what was happening, he'd been grabbed and was being held in somebody's arms. Barley was terrified! Oh, what's she going to do with me?

He'd heard dreadful stories about
people-folk and rabbits. They put rabbits
in a pie, whatever that is. Then they
eat them! This is the end! I'll never see
Mellow, Bramble, Bracken, Berry, Fern or
Wisher again!

The dog sat on the grass and looked
up at him. Then Barley saw it was Sasha.
He remembered she'd chased Bracken
and Wisher once. Sasha recognised
Barley too.

"Sorry, Barley!" she said. "I didn't
know it was you. My mistress is very cross
with me."

"Hm!" said Barley. "I never have and
never will trust dogs!"

He was shaking.

"You poor rabbit!" said Jenny
Fairweather, giving him a cuddle. "Let's
find your owner, shall we?"

"Oh, no!" said Sasha to Barley. "Jenny
thinks you're someone's pet! She doesn't
know you live in the wild."

Barley tried to wriggle free, but Jenny
was holding him tight. She hurried across
to the show ring with Sasha trotting
obediently at her heels.

Barley peered over Jenny's arms.
He saw Daisy Duck flapping her wings
and quacking.

"Poor Barley Longears!"

Quack, quack, quack!

Fred Fairweather had just finished
judging eight dogs in the Tail-Wagging
competition. He'd awarded First Prize to
Toby, who looked very pleased. Toby
was still wagging his tail! Fred was
getting ready to judge the rabbits in the
show, when he saw Jenny coming into
the ring with another rabbit. She put
Barley down inside a small enclosure.

Barley was scared and confused. He ran around, looking for a way to escape through the wire netting. But there were no holes to crawl through and the sides were too high for him to jump. There were lots of other rabbits in the enclosure all looking at him in surprise.

I don't understand why I'm the only rabbit trying to get out of here, thought Barley. Silly rabbits! What are they waiting for? I must go home. Mellow will be worrying her whiskers off! And Wisher! Oh, I hope she's all right.

It was then that a rabbit with droopy ears – the one Barley had seen earlier – hopped over and spoke to him:

"Hello," he said. "I'm Nigel."

Nigel? Barley thought the name sounded familiar. Oh, yes! I remember.

"I think you met two of my children, once," he told Nigel. "Bracken and Wisher Longears."

"Yes!" said Nigel happily. "They rescued me from the Dark Forest. Bracken and Wisher were very kind. They helped me find my mistress, Abby."

"I'm Barley Longears," said Barley.

"Nice to meet you, Barley," said Nigel.

"I'm hoping to win a prize today. Abby would be pleased. I love pet shows, don't you?"

Barley didn't know what a prize was, or a pet show, and he wasn't sure he wanted to find out.

"Er, no," he said. "I've had a terrible day! I can't wait to get back to my burrow."

"Oh," said Nigel. "I suppose this is all a bit strange for you. Bracken told me you live underground. I wouldn't like that. I live in a cage. I have a straw bed and Abby brings me Nutty Nibbles, which is my favourite food."

Barley was only half-listening.

He had noticed a man looking carefully at each rabbit in turn. And now the man was bending down, looking straight at him. Oh, help! thought Barley. He's going to put me in a pie and eat me!

"What a fine rabbit!" said Fred, tickling Barley under the chin. "Glossy coat. Bright eyes. Long ears! I think this one deserves a prize."

Then Fred hung a tiny medal on a red ribbon around Barley's neck.

"Congratulations!" said Fred, giving Barley a pat. "Best Rabbit in Show!"

Barley blinked. He didn't know what to make of it.

"Who does he belong to, Jenny?" said Fred.

"I don't know," said Jenny. "He's lost his owner."

"Never mind," said Fred. "I'll make an announcement over the loudspeaker. Someone is sure to claim him."

"LADIES AND GENTLEMEN, BOYS AND GIRLS, MAY I HAVE YOUR ATTENTION? WOULD THE OWNER OF A BLACK AND WHITE RABBIT WITH UNUSUALLY LONG EARS PLEASE COME TO THE SHOW RING AND COLLECT HIM. HE HAS JUST WON BEST RABBIT IN SHOW!"

When no one came forward to collect Barley, Fred continued judging the competition.

He awarded Nigel a prize for the
Longest Droopy Ears!

Nigel's owner, Abby, was delighted
when Fred presented her with a silky,
blue rosette to hang on Nigel's cage.

"Thank you," said Abby.

A little earlier, she had noticed Nigel
and Barley together. They seemed to be
getting on very well, and she wondered
if Nigel would like another rabbit to keep
him company. She thought Barley looked
very handsome too. Abby pointed to him.
"Please, Mr Fairweather. If that rabbit
doesn't belong to anyone, may I take
him? There's plenty of room in Nigel's
cage for two rabbits!"

"Good idea," said Fred. "He deserves
a good home."

Barley pricked his ears. He didn't like the sound of that at all. And when Abby picked him up, Barley suddenly saw his chance to escape.

"I'm sorry, Nigel," he said. "It's nothing personal. I'm off!"

Barley kicked, struggled and squirmed with all his strength, until Abby couldn't hold him any more.

"Oh!" she cried, and let go.

Barley leapt to the ground. He ran and ran as fast as his legs could carry him and didn't stop until he reached the riverbank.

"Phew!" said Barley, panting. His heart was beating fast. He looked for Daisy Duck, but couldn't see her anywhere. He turned around and, to his horror, he saw people-folk rushing towards the river.

"They're after me!" cried Barley. "I can't wait for Daisy. I have to go."

Barley knew he needed to follow the river home, so he turned left. It was then he saw the ducks.

They were bright yellow, all about
the same size, and bobbing about on the
water. Barley's eyes popped.

"This must be the Duck Race Daisy
told me about," he said. "I've never seen
so many ducks in my life!"

The Duck Race
5

News of Barley spread along the riverbank like wildfire. After Daisy had seen Barley carried away by Jenny Fairweather, she'd hurried to tell someone. The first friend she met was Violet Vole.

"Barley Longears is in trouble!" quacked Daisy. "Hazel Heron was fishing up-river and thought Barley was going to attack her. It was all a big mistake, of course, but Hazel flew Barley to

Fairweather's and dropped him in the duck pond! As if that wasn't bad enough, poor Barley was chased by Sasha the sheepdog, then caught by his mistress and carried away."

"What a terrible tale!" said Violet.

She watched Daisy go back
up-river towards Fairweather's, then
hurried to find someone to talk to. Violet
couldn't wait to pass on the story! The
first friend she met was Sylvia Squirrel.

"Have you heard?" said Violet. "Barley
is up to his ears in trouble this morning!
He was nearly caught by
some sheep in the river.
I think that's right? Then
Hazel Heron thought
Barley was a fish and
tried to eat him!

A big mistake, of course. He just got away, but was spotted by two enormous dogs. Or were there three? The dogs chased Barley into a duck pond at Fairweather's, then someone called Sasha flew off with him!"

"What a dreadful story!" said Sylvia. "I must go and tell Mellow at once."

Sylvia found Mellow with Bramble, Bracken, Berry, Fern and Wisher outside their burrow. Everyone looked very worried.

"I really don't know how to begin," said Sylvia. "Maybe you've heard? Barley is in dreadful trouble! Such a worry for you all. An extraordinary story!

Daisy Duck saw everything. She told Violet Vole and Violet told me, although Violet may have got things a bit muddled. You know how she gets confused . . ."

"PLEASE, Sylvia!" said Mellow. "Tell us what's happened."

"Well," said Sylvia. "Barley met some sheep who tried to eat him! Then Hazel Heron – she's the new bird who arrived this morning and lives by the river. Have you seen her? Very long beak and legs. Anyway, Hazel was frightened and chased Barley all the way to Fairweather's duck pond. Poor Barley fell in and six enormous dogs went in after him. Then a flying-fish called Sasha carried him away!"

Mellow's eyes opened wide. She stared at Sylvia, not knowing what to believe. Earlier that morning, Bramble, Bracken, Berry, Fern and Wisher had told her quite a different story. The young rabbits told Sylvia what they'd seen down by the little wooden bridge.

"Hazel Heron flew off with Parr," said Bramble.

"After Burdock tried to attack me," said Wisher.

"He came between Burdock and Wisher," said Bracken.

"Yes," said Wisher. "Parr scared Burdock away. He was so brave!"

"Then he fell into the river," said Berry.

"Poor Parr!" said Fern. "We'll never see him again. He's gone for EVER!"

Mellow tried to comfort Fern, even though she was worried herself.

"We don't know that," she said. "Your parr is a very clever rabbit! He can look after himself. I'm sure he'll be home soon." Then to Sylvia, "Thank you, Sylvia. We were about to search for Barley, but didn't know where to start. From what you say, it sounds as though we should go in the direction of the Farm Park."

"You can try," said Sylvia. "But I fear you may be too late!"

Just then, Mellow saw that Wisher looked puzzled.

"What is it?" she said.

"My ears," said Wisher. "While you were talking, they began to tingle. I can hear a voice inside my head. It's about Parr!"

"What does it say?" said the others.
Wisher told them:

"Wisher, Wisher, come and see
Barley by the fallen tree!"

"Oh, my whiskers!" said Mellow. "We must go to him at once."

Daisy was anxiously looking out for Barley along the river. She hoped he'd escaped from Fairweather's. If not, she would go back to the Farm Park and find out what had happened.

Daisy had never forgotten the
day Mellow Longears had saved her
ducklings when they were in danger.
Now she wanted to help Barley too. She
hoped her urgent message had reached
Mellow. Maybe Mellow would send a
search party?

Daisy was swimming near the old
tree, which had fallen across the water.

She was trying to go up-stream, but the river was flowing faster than usual and she struggled against the current. Daisy was just coming round a bend when she got a big surprise. There were ducks as far as she could see. Yellow ducks with red beaks and staring eyes – just like the ones she'd seen at the Farm Park.

Only now there were so many that Daisy couldn't even begin to count them!

The fast-moving river was carrying the ducks towards her at an alarming speed. Daisy paddled fast with her webbed feet, but she couldn't get out of their way.

"Quack, quack, quack!" cried Daisy. "Help!"

At that moment, Barley came running along a path. He heard the frantic sound of quacking.

"That sounds like Daisy," he said, pausing for a moment to listen. "I wonder what's wrong?"

Barley had thought the yellow ducks that were swimming silently in the river beside him very strange. He couldn't understand why none of them spoke.

Not one had opened its beak since the start of the Duck Race! Barley had watched the ducks set off, then kept pace with them along the way. Once, when he paused for a moment to rest in the long grass, he saw a duck bobbing near the bank.

"Hello," said Barley. The duck ignored him and swam on. "Huh! Well, I don't have time to worry about silly ducks anyway! I must hurry or the people-folk will catch me."

Suddenly, Barley heard a cry for help. It was Daisy. He saw her down-river, paddling against the strong current.

She was facing a fleet of yellow ducks, and was being swept backwards towards the fallen log. Oh, buttercups! thought Barley. Soon Daisy will be trapped between the tree and those horrid ducks. I must do something!

"Coming, Daisy!" he cried.

Back to the Burrow!
6

Mellow led her search party towards the river. As she ran, she wondered about Wisher's message:

"Wisher, Wisher, come and see
Barley by the fallen tree!"

Mellow knew exactly where to go.

It was an old tree that had blown down
in a storm, many moons ago. It had
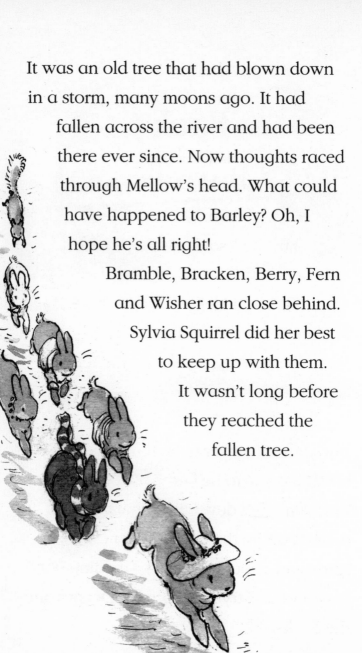
fallen across the river and had been
there ever since. Now thoughts raced
through Mellow's head. What could
have happened to Barley? Oh, I
hope he's all right!

Bramble, Bracken, Berry, Fern
and Wisher ran close behind.
Sylvia Squirrel did her best
to keep up with them.
It wasn't long before
they reached the
fallen tree.

"Parr! Parr!" shouted Bramble.

"I can't see him anywhere," said Bracken.

"Nor can I," said Berry.

"Are you sure this is the right tree, Wisher?" said Fern.

"It must be," said Wisher. "There's only one . . ."

"Look!" said Mellow. "There he is!"

Barley could never quite remember how he came to be in the water for the third time that day. One minute he was rushing along the path. Next, he was splashing about in the river, holding out his paws and trying to protect Daisy from the ducks.

From somewhere above his head, he
heard shouting:

"Barley!"

"Parr!"

"Here!"

"Ooo! Be careful!"

"Well done!"

"Mind the ducks!"

Barley looked up. He couldn't believe
his eyes. Standing on the fallen tree-trunk
were Mellow, Bramble, Bracken, Berry,
Fern and Wisher. Sylvia Squirrel and
Violet Vole were waving from the bank.

"Caw, caw, caw!" said Craggs and
Clary Crow from their nest in the big oak.

Then, from the corner of his eye,
Barley saw Hazel Heron standing
in the river.

"Let me help you, Barley," said Hazel.
She lifted Barley by one ear with her
beak, and placed him gently on the path.

"Thank you," said Barley. He hadn't expected to meet Hazel again quite so soon, but he was very pleased to see her. She's not so bad, after all! he thought.

"That's all right, Barley," said Hazel. "Always glad to help a friend. Now, I think Daisy needs my help too."

Barley watched Hazel wade back out into the middle of the river. She stood on one of her very long, thin legs, and pushed aside some yellow ducks with the other. Daisy swam to safety.

"Quack, quack, quack!" said Daisy happily.

"Hooray!" everyone cheered.

Some people-folk had gathered nearby. Barley looked at them warily. He was sure they would catch him now.

But they seemed too busy with the funny yellow ducks and the Duck Race to bother about him. Barley watched them scooping up the ducks from the river and carrying them away.

"I'll never understand people-folk," he said to Mellow as they hopped home together. "A little girl wanted to keep me in a cage. And those people-folk were putting ducks in a box!"

100

Back at the burrow, Barley sat with
his family trying to remember everything
that had happened to him. Sylvia Squirrel
and Violet Vole were there too. They
wanted to hear the whole story!

Barley looked around at Bramble,
Bracken, Berry, Fern and Wisher.

"I couldn't stop worrying about you,"
he said. "I was so afraid Burdock . . .
Wisher . . ."

"You were brilliant, Parr!" said Wisher. "Burdock got the fright of his life when you charged at him."

"Ah, yes," said Barley. "That's when I fell in the water for the first time. I've been in and out of rivers and duck ponds all day!"

"And up in the air," said Bramble. "We saw you fly off with Hazel."

"Er, yes," said Barley. "That was very scary. Flying is definitely not for me."

Just then, Mellow noticed something shiny and round on Barley's chest. When his coat had been wet, she hadn't spotted it. Now that his fur was dry, she could see it glinting in the sunshine.

"What's that?" Mellow said.

"Oh, something I was given at the Pet Show," said Barley. "I tried to take it off, but I couldn't get it over my head."

"What's it for?" said Fern.

"A prize, I think they said," said Barley. "Best Rabbit in Show or something."

Mellow smiled. After all Barley had been through that day, she knew just what his prize was for.

"Best Rabbit in Show?" she said. "No, Barley Longears. Best Rabbit Ever!"

Author's Note

The view from my cottage window overlooking the Kensey Valley, North Cornwall, and the Launceston Steam Railway were my inspiration for writing *The Railway Rabbits*. The route of the railway, which runs along this unspoilt river valley, links the once ancient capital of Cornwall with New Mills Farm Park and provided me with the perfect setting for my adventurous rabbits.

I began my research in January 2010, by visiting the owners of the railway, Kay and Nigel Bowman. Sitting in the Station Café they told me about their railway and some of the weird and wonderful things they'd seen, whilst driving the trains.

Yes, Kay is a train driver too! And I rode on the footplate of a bright, red locomotive called Covertcoat, which became my inspiration for the Red Dragon. The idea for the first book, *Wisher and the Runaway Piglet*, was based on a real pig that had wandered on to the line. I'm not sure if that pig was carried home on the train, but it makes a good story!

The stories are told mostly from the rabbit's point of view and, from this perspective, these are big adventures for little rabbits. I've tried to convey a sense of reality about the dangers rabbits face living in the wild – the Longears' number one enemy is Burdock the buzzard. I often see one of these magnificent birds circling overhead, or sitting on a telegraph pole in our meadow.

I hope you enjoy reading all the books in this series as much as I've enjoyed writing them. My thanks to my family and the many people who have helped me along the way. I'm particularly grateful to Kay and Nigel Bowman at Launceston Steam Railway; to Richard and Sandra Ball at New Mills Farm Park; my agent, Rosemary Sandberg and everyone at Orion Children's Books, with special thanks to my publisher, Fiona Kennedy; editor Jenny Glencross; designers Loulou Clark and Abi Hartshorne, and to Anna Currey for her wonderful illustrations.

Georgie Adams
Cornwall, 2014

www.georgieadams.com
www.orionbooks.co.uk

Look out for . . .
Wisher and the Noisy Crows

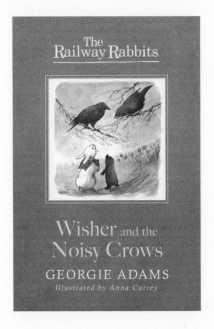

Join the Railway Rabbits: Barley, Mellow,
Bramble, Bracken, Berry, Fern and Wisher
Longears in their adventures.

A family of noisy crows has arrived on the riverbank –
their home has been destroyed! When Wisher sets off to
find out what's happened, everyone is in for a big surprise.

978 1 4440 1223 1
£4.99

the orion star

★ ★ ★

CALLING ALL GROWN-UPS!
Sign up for **the orion star** newsletter to
hear about your favourite authors and exclusive
competitions, plus details of how children
can join our 'Story Stars' review panel.

Sign up at:

www.orionbooks.co.uk/orionstar

Follow us 🐦 @the_orionstar
Find us 📘 facebook.com/TheOrionStar